The Time Machine

H. G. WELLS

SADDLEBACK
PUBLISHING · INC.

Saddleback's *Illustrated Classics*™

Three Watson
Irvine, CA 92618-2767
Website: www.sdlback.com

ISBN 1-56254-944-8

Printed in China.

Welcome to
Saddleback's *Illustrated Classics*™

We are proud to welcome you to Saddleback's *Illustrated Classics*™. Saddleback's *Illustrated Classics*™ was designed specifically for the classroom to introduce readers to many of the great classics in literature. Each text, written and adapted by teachers and researchers, has been edited using the Dale-Chall vocabulary system. In addition, much time and effort has been spent to ensure that these high-interest stories retain all of the excitement, intrigue, and adventure of the original books.

With these graphically *Illustrated Classics*™, you learn what happens in the story in a number of different ways. One way is by reading the words a character says. Another way is by looking at the drawings of the character. The artist can tell you what kind of person a character is and what he or she is thinking or feeling.

This series will help you to develop confidence and a sense of accomplishment as you finish each novel. The stories in Saddleback's *Illustrated Classics*™ are fun to read. And remember, fun motivates!

Overview

Everyone deserves to read the best literature our language has to offer. Saddleback's *Illustrated Classics*™ was designed to acquaint readers with the most famous stories from the world's greatest authors, while teaching essential skills. You will learn how to:

- Establish a purpose for reading
- Use prior knowledge
- Evaluate your reading
- Listen to the language as it is written
- Extend literary and language appreciation through discussion and writing activities

Reading is one of the most important skills you will ever learn. It provides the key to all kinds of information. By reading the *Illustrated Classics*™, you will develop confidence and the self-satisfaction that comes from accomplishment— a solid foundation for any reader.

Step-By-Step

The following is a simple guide to using and enjoying each of your *Illustrated Classics*™. To maximize your use of the learning activities provided, we suggest that you follow these steps:

1. ***Listen!*** We suggest that you listen to the read-along. (At this time, please ignore the beeps.) You will enjoy this wonderfully dramatized presentation.

2. ***Pre-reading Activities.*** After listening to the audio presentation, the pre-reading activities in the Activity Book prepare you for reading the story by setting the scene, introducing more difficult vocabulary words, and providing some short exercises.

3. ***Reading Activities.*** Now turn to the "While you are reading" portion of the Activity Book, which directs you to make a list of story-related facts. Read-along while listening to the audio presentation. (This time pay attention to the beeps, as they indicate when each page should be turned.)

4. ***Post-reading Activities.*** You have successfully read the story and listened to the audio presentation. Now answer the multiple-choice questions and other activities in the Activity Book.

Remember,

"Today's readers are tomorrow's leaders."

H. G. Wells

Herbert George Wells, an English novelist, historian, journalist, and author of science-fiction stories, was born in 1866. His father was a shopkeeper, and his mother worked occasionally as a housekeeper. After completing his early formal schooling, Wells worked as a teacher. He later received a scholarship to study at a school with a special focus on the sciences.

His training as a scientist is shown in his imaginative science-fiction stories. Wells described trips in airplanes and submarines when such modes of transportation had not yet been invented. *The Time Machine* describes a trip into the future, and *The War of the Worlds* is an account of an invasion from Mars. Several of his science fiction works have been the basis of popular movies.

Though he is best-known for his science fiction stories, Wells wrote a variety of other works. He was a strong believer in education and wrote three lengthy books in which he tried to bring important ideas in history and science to the general public. His numerous books, articles, and essays also show his bold support of social change.

H. G. Wells died in 1946.

Saddleback's *Illustrated Classics*™

The Time Machine

H. G. WELLS

THE MAIN CHARACTERS

Eloi

Weena

Time Traveller

Morlocks

Professors

*My invention had worked. Here I am in the world of the future.
I wondered what it would be like. My Time Machine had carried
me thousands of years beyond the time in which I lived. I am
going to explore the world and its people in the year 802,701 A.D.*

Just call me the Time Traveller. The year is 1896. I have the most unbelievable story to tell, yet every word is true. I am an inventor and one night I invited some friends over to make an important announcement. But first I had to explain something....

A line has one dimension. It has length. A square has two dimensions. It has length and height.

That's right.

A cube has three dimensions. It has length, height, and thickness.

It's solid, you can hold it.

A cube lasts over a period of time, so there must be a fourth dimension...time.

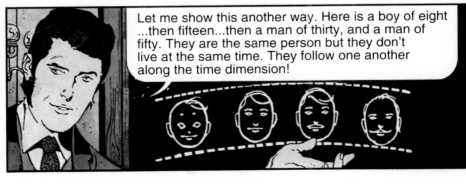

Let me show this another way. Here is a boy of eight ...then fifteen...then a man of thirty, and a man of fifty. They are the same person but they don't live at the same time. They follow one another along the time dimension!

Time dimension? We have known only three dimensions for years!

Have we? Up until the invention of the balloon, man lived in a flat world, in two dimensions. Only the balloon, rising upward, gave us three dimensions.

Then came my shocking tale.

Since we only recently discovered or used the third dimension, maybe we have also not tried to travel through the fourth dimension of time, into the past or future.

Travel through time?

Of all the wild, stupid ideas!

But I was prepared to back up my idea.

This is only a model of my travelling machine! And it works!

Surely, you're joking!

I asked one of them to come forward and....

The black lever is for stopping. But press that tiny white lever for the future and you will see what happens. It is already becoming invisible as it leaves time and....

....disappears into the future!

My word!

It must be a trick!

I wasn't surprised when they didn't seem to believe it.

Bah! Some magic trick, that's all.

Any stage magician can do the same.

You don't believe me, gentlemen? Follow me to my workshop where I've almost finished a full sized Time Machine I will ride myself.

Look here! Are you perfectly serious?

I was never more serious in my life. I will travel through time! Those dials will show me the days, weeks months, and years as I travel into the past or future!

I knew they wouldn't believe me but I invited them to return in one week.

I'll be back from my time trip then, and you'll hear the story!

Fiddle-sticks!

You should be a fairy tale writer, not an inventor.

The next morning, I busily tuned up the machine, oiled it carefully, and set the dials for zero. But I must say I was worried.

Even though the model disappeared how do I know it really followed the time dimension into the future. Well, I'll soon find out!

Trembling in excitement, I sat in the machine.

As a trial, I'll just pull the future lever a short ways.

A moment of dizziness ....of spinning around....

My head is spinning! I'll turn the other dial and stop myself quickly.

Everything straightened out, but I was disappointed.

Everything looks the same. Did anything happen? Maybe my invention is a failure?

Wait! The clock shows almost 3:30! It was about 10:00 a moment ago!

Then I did travel into the future for...five and a half hours! All so quickly. It works!

Eagerly, I turned the future dial again for a longer trip, and I saw a strange thing happen!

My housekeeper came in and went out the back door, moving like a rocket! That means time is passing at high speed for me!

Then everything around me changed, and I could hardly believe what I saw.

Heavens! It's like moving through a strange universe. It's all so strange ... as if I'm being turned inside out.

But then I got hold of my nerves and came out of my dizzy spell.

It seems sometime in the near future the building I lived in is being torn down. I'm entering the open air even though I'm standing still.

Able to see around now, I saw still more unbelievable things as the days spun by at greater and greater speed.

Day and night are passing so swiftly that the sun and moon look like long streaks of light, as they circle the turning earth!

It looks like the land the house stood on was turned into a park. Trees are growing up as fast as weeds; the years are spinning by now!

Now I see a future city with beautiful towers around me! But it's fading away quickly as I keep moving into the time zones ahead!

How could I ever tell about all the great cities of the future I saw so quickly, each better than the last? But there were also terrible happenings as the calendar went far beyond my nineteenth century.

In my "sight-seeing" tour of the future, I forgot my time dials and when I thought of stopping....

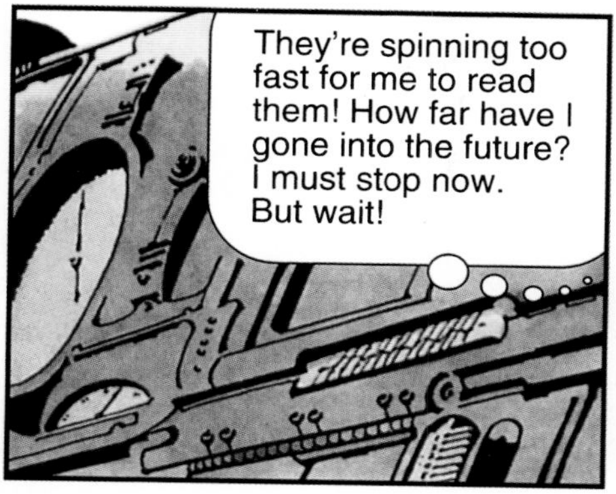
They're spinning too fast for me to read them! How far have I gone into the future? I must stop now. But wait!

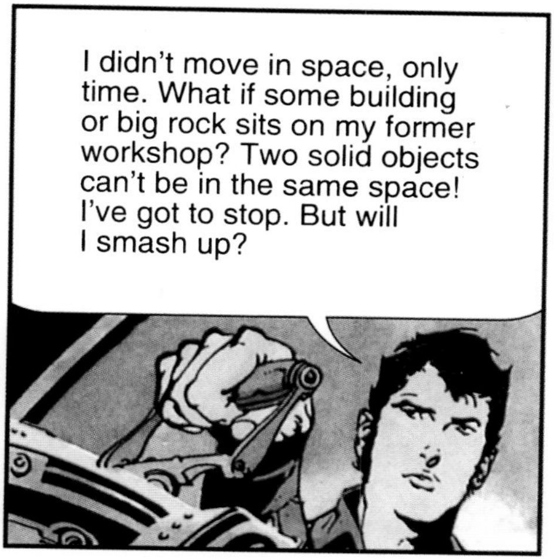
I didn't move in space, only time. What if some building or big rock sits on my former workshop? Two solid objects can't be in the same space! I've got to stop. But will I smash up?

Suddenly I was flying through space.

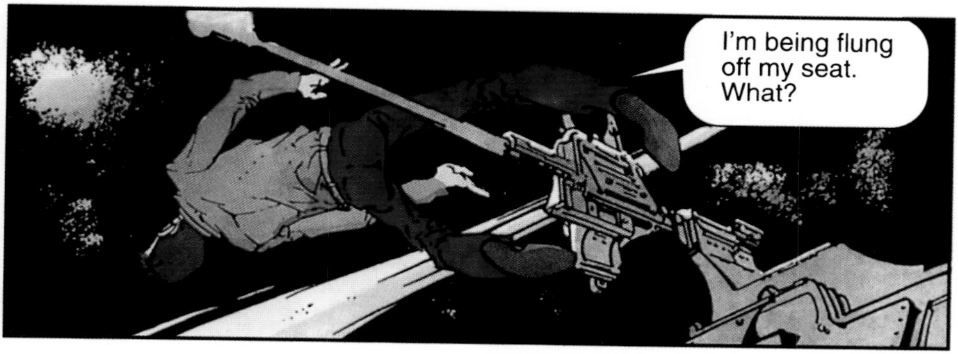
I'm being flung off my seat. What?

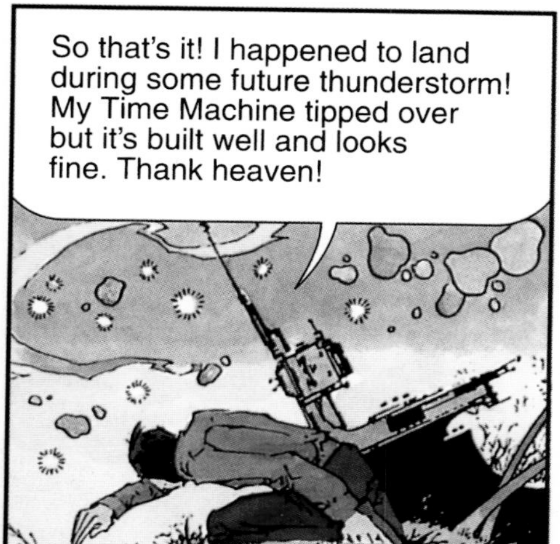
So that's it! I happened to land during some future thunderstorm! My Time Machine tipped over but it's built well and looks fine. Thank heaven!

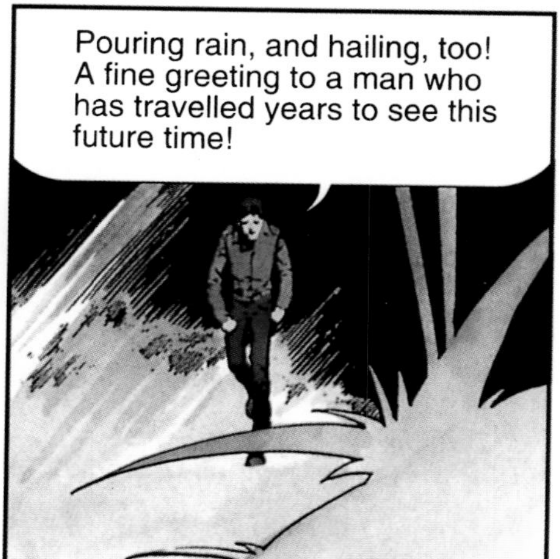
Pouring rain, and hailing, too! A fine greeting to a man who has travelled years to see this future time!

As the rain and hail began to clear, I stared at something strange nearby.

I see other giant buildings through the rain! How do I know who lives in them? I don't belong here in the far future!

Yes, fear took hold of me at this strange changing scene! I ran to my Time Machine, and....

....turned it upright.

Got to leave this strange future time I know nothing about!

It was then I looked at the dial readings and received the shock of my life!

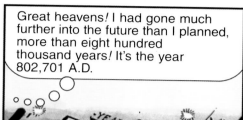

Great heavens! I had gone much further into the future than I planned, more than eight hundred thousand years! It's the year 802,701 A.D.

I had all the more reason for wanting to leave quickly.

But I stopped for a moment when I heard strange musical voices.

People here after all! Well, I may as well see what the future folk look like.

Why, they're only four feet tall. They must be teenagers, not adults. They act gay and happy. No weapons, so I'm in no danger.

And at sight of these friendly creatures, I suddenly lost my fears and took my hands from the controls.

They speak in a strange, sweet musical language. Hmm, now they're feeling me all over wondering whether I'm real!

But I made a sudden motion to warn them when I saw their little hands feeling the Time Machine.

I had better remove the two control dials so that they can't accidentally make it work and leave me stranded here!

Then I carefully looked at their faces more closely.

They're as pretty as Dresden dolls, both the boys and girls.

I decided to try talking with them by using my hands.

To explain my Time Machine how do I show time? I'll point at the sun which moves daily and marks off days... they don't understand.

One little girl then repeated my movements and at the same time....

She's making the sound of thunder! But why?

Can it be that they are not very smart and that they ask me a childish question? Did I come from the sun in a thunderstorm?

I nodded helplessly and then, to my surprise....

Why, they're all bowing to me! Good Lord, I hope they won't worship me as a god of thunder and lightning!

But then they were all running to and fro for flowers, and cheerfully throwing them upon me until I was almost covered with blossoms.

They are just like children. They change from game to game at a moment's notice.

And they next led me to a large grey building of rough stone, and into a large hallway with a strangely carved ceiling.

The big doorway opened into a big hall, filled with long, low, stone tables on which rested big bowls of fruit.

Looks like their dining hall. They sit on cushions on the floor.

Stained-glass windows...colorful drapes...it all looks rich and like a picture.

I tried to figure out why they were vegetarians.

Seems they are all vegetarians.* Odd fruits but they're delicious.

I bet that most or all animals are extinct today. Even in my time, man's hunting wiped out whole kinds of animals.

*Vegetarians are people who eat no meat—only fruit and vegetables.

After my hunger had disappeared, I tried to learn their speech.

I'll hold up a fruit and point. Ah, that boy gave its name. I'll try to repeat it in their language.

My first attempts to make the exquisite sounds of their language caused a great amount of laughter!

The world was quiet as I came out of the hall in the setting sun.

The world today is so different from the nineteenth century! It all seems like a parkland, filled with pretty flowers. And there have been changes in the land. The Thames River,* I see, is perhaps a mile from where it was in my time!

*A famous river in England.

As I walked on, I saw a pretty little building.

It's like a well under a dome! How odd!

I found a seat of some yellow metal, rusted in places, and I sat and looked at this view of the future world.

So many of the buildings here are empty and not ever used. It seems to me that the number of people on earth is going down.

The air is free of bugs, the earth is free of weeds. There are fruits and beautiful flowers everywhere. Colorful butterflies fly here and there. A garden world! It's beautiful!

But the people are so small with just the intelligence of children. The number of people on earth is getting smaller and even this beautiful land has places in ruins.

And there are so many less people on earth here in the future. No wars, no sickness, no wild animals to kill them off. They must plan to keep their numbers small.

What I thought *was* possible. But I would later find out I was very wrong!

As I returned to the spot where I had landed, something seemed wrong.

There's the White Sphinx on its base of bronze, the silver birch trees, the bushes, just like before. But is this the right place?

Where is my Time Machine? It's gone!

Suddenly I was frightened. Would I be here in the future forever...never able to get back to my own time. I began to hunt for the machine....

Have they moved it a little...pushed it under the bushes out of the way?

Then I stopped short. Above me stood the Sphinx...it seemed to smile and laugh at my fear.

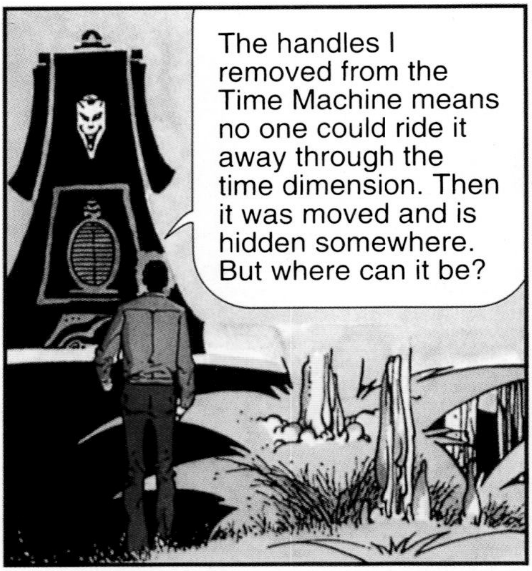
The handles I removed from the Time Machine means no one could ride it away through the time dimension. Then it was moved and is hidden somewhere. But where can it be?

I went wild as night fell, searching the bushes around the Sphinx, crying with anger and sadness.

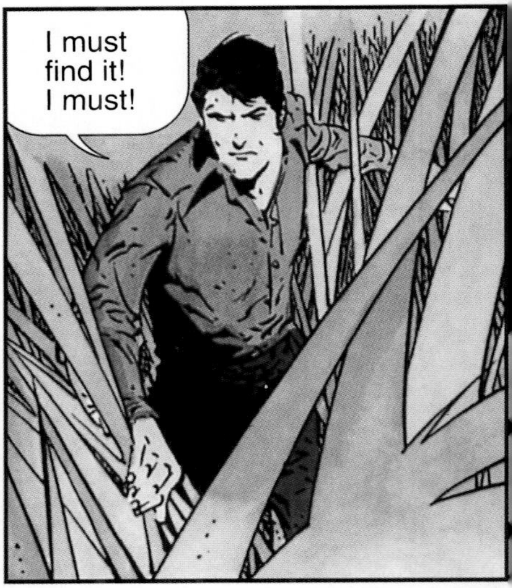
I must find it! I must!

In my fear, I even ran to the great stone building and found a second big hall where the little people slept. I lit a match in the dark and....

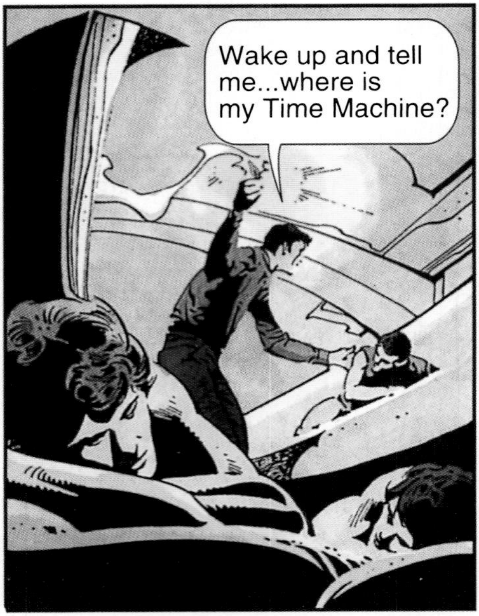
Wake up and tell me...where is my Time Machine?

I heard cries of fright behind me as I ran out again into the moonlight.

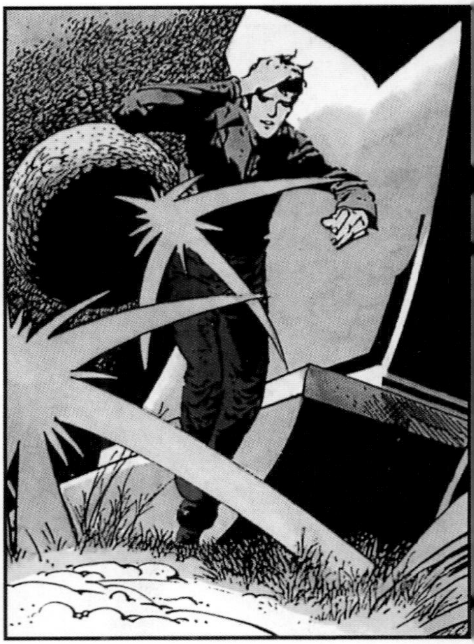

I felt hopelessly cut off from my own kind...a strange animal in an unknown world.

Good God, I'll be stuck here in the future, if I don't find my Time Machine!

Then I slept, and when I woke again it was daytime.

How did I get here? Wait... I remember now ...my machine is gone...last night I searched.

With the daylight, I began to think over my nightmare.

When some of the gay little people came by, I tried to talk to them using my hands.

Suppose the worst? Suppose the machine is lost...perhaps destroyed? It is necessary for me to be calm, to learn the way of the people, to get a clear idea of the means of getting materials and tools...so that in the end I can make another Time Machine! Simple as that!

They don't understand! They either have no feelings, or are laughing at me as if it were a joke.

Then I made a careful examination of the ground, and...

I came upon another strange clue.....

Ah, a groove cut in the lawn between the Sphinx's base and the marks of my feet where I had tried to move the overturned machine.

Narrow footprints like those made by an animal.

I went to the Sphinx and its bronze base, where the groove and footprints led.

Hmm, this base sounds hollow. If these panels are doors, they have no handles or keyholes, and must open toward the inside.

Well, I bet that my Time Machine is inside that base! But how it got there is a different problem!

When I tried to explain to the little folk, my wish to open the base doors, they seemed frightened.

They don't want to understand. They don't want to go near the base.

As another person turned away as if he didn't care about my problem, my temper got the better of me!

I'll drag him to the Sphinx and...No ...No...There's fear in his face! I'll let him go.

Instead, I returned and banged my fist at the bronze panels.

I hear something moving inside! And is that the sound of a laugh?

Angrily, I left and got a stone and hammered the doors with it.

This is only marking the decoration on the doors and green rust is coming off in powdery flakes! But no answer within!

Then I gave myself a talking to.

If you want your machine again, you must leave the Sphinx alone. Try to help yourself in other ways. Face this world and learn its ways. In the end you will find clues to it all.

In the following days I learned their language as well as I could....

....and in addition I explored here and there.

So far as I can see all the world here in the future has the same richness of the Thames Valley where I arrived. Beautiful buildings, lakes shining like silver, lovely trees. It's all very beautiful and calm.

There was something strange about all those round wells with covers over them. But when I went to look down into one using a match for light....

It must be very deep. I can see no gleam of water, nor my reflection.

But the way the matches act, there is a steady current of air going downward. And I hear a thud, thud, thud...like the beating of a big engine.

After a time, I came to connect these wells with tall towers standing here and there.

This strongly suggests a system of underground ventilation.

During the walks, I could see no signs of cemeteries nor anything that looked like tombs.

The thing that really puzzles me is that there are no old and weak among these people!

Another puzzle! The several big palaces I've explored were just dining rooms and places for sleeping. I can find no machinery of any kind. Who makes their fine clothes and all other things? There are no signs of workshops.

One day, I was watching some of the little people bathing, when suddenly....

A girl has a cramp and is drifting downstream in that swift stream! Yet none of her friends are making any attempt to rescue her!

I hurriedly took off my clothes.

I'll have to save her myself, if no one else will.

I caught the poor little girl before she went under for the last time. I'll bring her safely to land. But all those little people watching don't seem to care. They are not even upset that this girl almost drowned. Hard to believe!

A little rubbing of the arms soon brought her back to normal.

Her friends don't seem to care about her being saved. Her death would not have caused any worry. And of course I do not expect any thanks from the girl either.

In that, however, I was wrong! In the afternoon, when I returned from my walks, she greeted me with cries of delight, and gave me many flowers.

I tried talking to her and found out her name was Weena.

Weena is kissing my hand now.

And that was the beginning of a friendship which lasted a week.

From then on she tried to follow me all over, like a friendly puppy, trusting me completely. Once, as a test, I made ugly faces at her, but....

She simply laughs at me. Have these people no fears at all?

But there was one fear she shared with all the others.

Darkness seems to be the one thing they fear. I've never seen them sleep outside, always inside those safe walls. Even Weena is upset because I won't join them.

It troubled her greatly, but in the end her love for me won out, and for five of the nights of our friendship, she slept close to me.

I awoke with a start in the middle of the night. Up the hill I thought I could see three ghostly white figures.

Who or what are they? I've seen them every night since I've been here.

Are they carrying away a body of some kind? There is some mystery here I know nothing about.

Those strange night figures were soon going to be on my mind all the time!

The night seemed to be solid blackness. Suddenly I stopped.

But the creature left me and further on....

It's like a human spider! It's climbing down the wall on a ladder going down the shaft.

I suddenly realized the truth.

Mankind has divided into two different forms...the beautiful childlike creatures of the upperworld and the ugly nighttime creatures who live below.

As two of the beautiful Upperworld people came by, I pointed at the well and tried to ask a question about it .

They only seem worried, as if they fear the underworld creatures.

Leaving the ruins, my mind was filled with wonder.

There must be many tunnels under this ground where the new race lives. Those air shafts and wells along the hills and everywhere, show the great number of those underground tunnels.

From Weena I learned the name of the underground people and of her people.

Morlocks? — Eloi.

When I tried to question Weena about the Morlocks, she shivered as if she were frightened, but I kept asking and....

She burst out crying! For some reason, the Eloi hate or fear the Morlocks! Another big mystery for me to solve.

Hmm, for lack of a name, I'll call it the Palace of Green Porcelain, I must explore it tomorrow morning.

My exploring led me to a huge green structure –larger than any I had seen.

But in the morning, I saw that my interest in the Green Porcelain Palace was a way of putting off what I had to do.

I was just trying to put this off, but I must go down into the underworld.

When Weena saw what I was going to do, she cried out, and....

Don't try to hold me back, little one! No matter what lies below, I must know what it is.

As I climbed down the small ladder not made for anyone my size and weight, one of the bars suddenly bent.

I'll be thrown off into the blackness below and have a bad fall!

For a minute I hung by one hand but finally got my footing and continued down.

Weena is so far above me. And below the sound of machinery is growing louder!

Oh, a tunnel! I'll go in here and rest for a while.

I don't know how long I rested. I woke up when a soft hand touched my face. I sat up and struck a match.

The same white creatures I saw running that night above. They seem to be running from the light.

I met others as I walked but as soon as I struck a match, they ran.

Wait! Don't run.

No use. They always run off into the darkness of the tunnels.

Later I entered a huge room filled with machines.

These machines must be the ventilation system that pump air into this underground world.

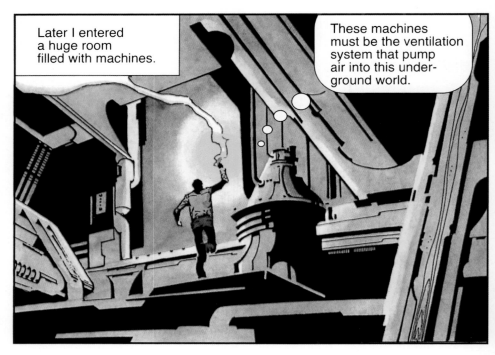

The smell of fresh blood filled the air and then I came upon....

A table, ready for a meal. The Morlocks eat meat at any rate!

I discovered that my supply of matches had run low.

Only four matches left. I should have brought more with me.

Each time a match had burned out before, the soft hands of the Morlocks had grabbed me. Frightened, I hurried back down the tunnel with the light of one of my matches.

They're after me. They want to bring me back.

When the first match burned out,
I lit the second, just in time.

How ugly and inhuman they look with those pale faces and those pink-gray eyes.

I used my third match to reach the ladder but as it burned out....

Morlocks grabbed my feet from behind...I'll be pulled back down.

I lit my last match and....

I've reached the ladder. Now I have to kick the Morlocks off so I can climb up!

The climb seems endless.
I feel sick...my head is spinning.
I hope I can make it.

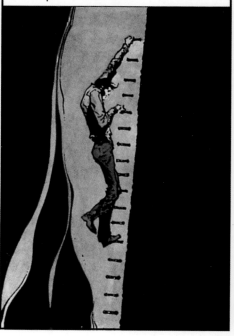

I got out of the well somehow and fell out into the blinding sunlight.

Even the soil smells sweet and clean up here! Weena is kissing my hands. She is so happy I'm back alive.

Now I understood one important thing about the world of 802,701 A.D.

The Eloi live in the bright Upperworld, while the Morlocks live in the dark Underworld and only come up at night. Both races show the signs of dying out. Both races are sliding downward.

Right away I decided to arm myself and find a place where I might sleep in safety away from the Morlocks!

I think I will explore the Palace of Green Porcelain as a hideaway.

On our way to the Green Palace, Weena picked two flowers and....

Weena! My pockets are not vases for flowers. Oh well, go ahead if it pleases you.

Night came before we reached the Green Palace, and as I looked up in the sky, I thought about what a great amount of time separated me from my nineteenth century.

The stars move slowly and all the ones that I knew are gone! The stars have moved themselves in new groupings! Even the Big Dipper is gone!

The next morning we found some fruit for our breakfast.

The Eloi only eat fruits. But I can't help remembering that meat I saw in the Morlock tunnel. Could it mean?

At some time in the past, the Morlock's food had run short. They had turned to eating other humans. The Morlocks are cannibals! The Eloi are just food for them.

Now it all makes sense! It is the Morlocks who make clothes for the Eloi, and all other things, while the poor Eloi dance and play all day! The Morlocks come up in the dark of night to steal Eloi and drag them below, to use as food.

When we found the Palace of Green Porcelain empty and falling into ruin....

Weena can't help me figure out those writings. The idea of writing is hardly known to the Eloi. Well, the door is broken open so we can enter.

It looked like a museum, with strange displays from ages that followed the nineteenth century, all unknown to me.

I stopped as I saw a machine with a handle sticking out.

Ah, just what I need, Weena! A club is more than enough, for any Morlock skull I might meet.

I found two other things of great value to me.

You don't know what I'm saying, Weena, but this is a box of matches, perfectly good, not even damp. And a sealed jar of fuel which burns very easily.

I was very much excited about finding weapons, until I saw their condition.

Guns of all kinds! But all rusted or cracked, just useless! I'll have to depend on my metal club.

Now, instead of looking for a hideaway, I changed my plans.

Come, Weena. With matches and fuel to fight off the Morlocks, let us return to the White Sphinx. Then I can use my iron bar and force open the Sphinx's doors and get my Time Machine.

As night fell and white shapes began to move around in the forest, I gathered firewood and built a fire to cover our escape.

There, Weena! With that fire behind us to drive the Morlocks back, we can go on safely for a good ways.

But as the campfire's glow died behind us....

The Morlocks are pulling at us. I must set Weena down and light a match.

That drove them back. But they'll close in again unless I light a block of fuel.

The fuel burned up and again drove the Morlocks back.

Now I'll pick up Weena and go on. She's so tired, poor thing.

But as the fire faded....

A Morlock trying to snatch Weena away.

When it was dark again and the Morlocks began creeping close, I reached for another match, but....

My matchbox, it's gone! They must have slipped it out of my pocket.

Then I was caught by the neck, by the arms...I felt as if I were in a huge spider's web.

The iron club in my hand gave me new strength and I found my way up, shaking the Morlocks from me.

I must use my club.

You Morlocks will have to fight harder to get me for your meat!

Suddenly, I saw a group of Morlocks running past me from behind....

The forest is on fire! My first fire is coming after me! It must have lit up dry grass and brush and started a big forest fire!

And now, I was afraid not of Morlocks attacking me, but in being run down by a mob of frightened creatures running from the fire. Morlocks kept running into me, and I had to use my club to clear the way as I too ran from the fire behind us.

Weena's gone!
I've got to find her...
out of my way,
you devils!

Though the fire could destroy the Morlocks, it also meant danger for me. And when I could not find Weena, I had to keep running to save myself from death by fire.

I finally stumbled to safety, but I was very upset.

My lovely Weena ...gone! The Morlocks captured her and they all died in the fire!

Sweet little Weena is no more! Well, I'm glad that she met her end in the fire...instead of the other way, underground!

The horrible death of Weena bothered me terribly. It left me alone again in this strange time... and at daybreak as I looked over the scene from a high point....

The White Sphinx! I must return there and find my Time Machine. Then I can leave this terrible time and return to my own.

I made a welcome discovery on the way.

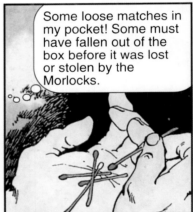

Some loose matches in my pocket! Some must have fallen out of the box before it was lost or stolen by the Morlocks.

The beauty of the people in the Upperworld covered the real ugliness of this world.

The Eloi lived a pleasant life, as pleasant as cattle in the field. Like cattle, they know of no enemies ...and their end is the same....killed for food!

It's sad to see how man stopped improving his mind. All man wanted was peace and comfort. It's as if his brain has died and only his body is still living.

Man must have gotten to feel safe and comfortable because he had no more problems to solve. The earth was quiet and at peace.

When man has no problems his mind isn't used. He doesn't think or plan. His mind just dies from lack of use. Man must use his mind if it is to continue growing.

Look at what happened. The people of the Upperworld are pretty but their minds are weak. The people of the Underworld live by stealing and eating their Upperworld neighbors.

Man can't grow or improve any more. They will become completely extinct in time. That's the year 802,701 A.D. in a nutshell.

After thinking about what had happened, I spent the night sleeping, then walked toward the Sphinx with my club in one hand while the other hand played with matches in my pocket. I found a surprise ....

The doors are open! They've been pushed to the side.

There's my Time Machine. After all my worry and planning and here it is!

I was surprised to find it had been carefully oiled and cleaned. I guessed what the Morlocks had been up to.

The Morlocks probably took it apart while they tried to figure out what it was for.

The thing I had expected suddenly happened. The bronze panels closed and locked me in.

I'm in the dark ...trapped! So the Morlocks think!

I laughed happily. I could hear their murmuring laughter, in turn, as they came towards me. Very calmly, I took out what they didn't know I still had.

Matches! The one thing that can drive them back.

But I was shocked as I tried to strike a match....

Good Lord! These matches are the kind that light only on their own box! They're useless this way!

I acted fast, pulling my two drive dials from my pocket and....

I'll knock them back and climb into the seat of my Time Machine

Now to fit the dials in place. Wait! A Morlock has got hold of one dial!

Quickly I punched the Morlock and heard his head crack.

Got it!

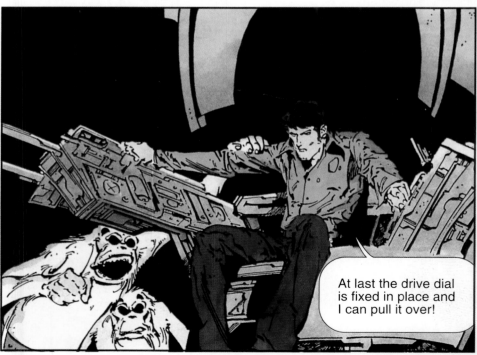

At last the drive dial is fixed in place and I can pull it over!

The Morlock hands slipped from me...I was on my way through the time dimension!

I was not seated right in the machine. For a long time I hung on as the machine swayed and shook.

As I drove on, the appearance of things around me changed.

All signs of the moon have gone and the sun streak is slowing down!

Now the sun has grown large and red, and has stopped motionless on the horizon. That means the earth has come to rest with one face to the sun!

I stopped the Time Machine to look at a strange world. The sky was Indian red. At a beach there were no waves. There was not a breath of wind.

The only sign of life is a coating of lichens, plants which grow in a little light.

But I was wrong.

A giant butterfly! And that crab-like creature is as big as a table!

I felt a tickling on my cheek, and when I tried to brush it away....

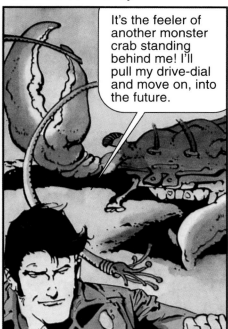

It's the feeler of another monster crab standing behind me! I'll pull my drive-dial and move on, into the future.

As I travelled on in great leaps of a thousand years or more, I stopped again and again....

The sun grows larger and duller, and the life of the old earth is dying away.

At last, more than thirty million years in the future, the huge red-hot ball of the sun had come to cover nearly a tenth of the sky.

White flakes are whirling down. The sea is full of ice. That green slime on rocks alone proves that life is not yet extinct...but close to it.

Suddenly I noticed an eclipse* of the large sun was beginning...

*A time when the sun is blocked from sight.

I could stand it no more and now turned my dials in the other direction.

The hands are spinning backward on the time dials. I'm returning to the past!

Now I see the dim shadows of buildings and future cities.

I'm almost back. I see our own nineteenth century's narrow and familiar buildings.

The old walls of my laboratory are forming around me. I'll slow down the time dial to zero.

I saw an odd thing, then....

I'm passing again across that minute when my house-keeper crossed the laboratory. But now her every move is the exact opposite of her earlier ones.

As I finally stopped the machine, my old workshop was around me again. I might have slept and dreamed my whole adventure!

My tools, just as I left them. No, wait... something is different.

I started my time trip from the southeast corner of my lab. But now it rests in the northwest corner. That gives the exact distance from where I landed on that lawn, to the platform in the White Sphinx, where the Morlocks had carried my machine!

In the hallway, I saw the date on Pall Mall's Gazette.

Exactly a week since I told my friends about going on a time trip. I hear their voices and the clatter of plates. They are here as I invited them, for Thursday dinner.

When I appeared in the doorway where my guests were dining....

Good heavens! Man, what's the matter?

What on earth have you been up to, man?

Ah, good champagne! Let me drink and eat before I tell my tale. And save me some of that lamb. I'm starving for a bit of meat.

Sorry, but I was simply starved. I've had a most amazing time. Most of it will sound like lying but it's true...every word of it. I've lived eight days... such days as no human being ever lived before! Here's the story.

When I had finished, there was silence for a long moment, then....

What a pity it is you're not a writer of stories!

You don't believe me? I thought not. I hardly believe it myself.

But then I drew the dying white flowers from my pocket and put them on the table.

And yet...what about these flowers? Examine them if you will.

Gynaeceum? But it's odd. I certainly don't know the natural order of these flowers. Where did you get them?

They were put into my pocket by Weena! Isn't that proof enough that I travelled into time? Dear Weena ...I'll never forget her.

They say life is a dream, a poor dream at times...I went back to my workshop after my guests left.

If it was a dream, where did it come from? I must find out.

Yes, I'm going on another time trip. Where? I don't know. Perhaps into the past, among the hairy savages of the Stone Age...or among the ugly lizards of the reptile age...or beside one of the lonely salt lakes of the Triassic Age.

But no...I'll go into the future again. I'll find Weena who proved that even though mankind was becoming extinct there was room for love in the heart of man.

I don't know if I'll ever come back... goodbye!

The End